John Norbury

The Box of Whistles

an illustrated book on organ cases - with notes on organs at home and

abroad

John Norbury

The Box of Whistles
an illustrated book on organ cases - with notes on organs at home and abroad

ISBN/EAN: 9783337340162

Printed in Europe, USA, Canada, Australia, Japan

Cover: Foto ©Andreas Hilbeck / pixelio.de

More available books at **www.hansebooks.com**

THE

BOX OF WHISTLES

AN ILLUSTRATED BOOK ON ORGAN CASES:

WITH

Notes on Organs at Home and Abroad.

BY

JOHN NORBURY.

LONDON:

BRADBURY, AGNEW, & CO., 8, 9, 10, BOUVERIE STREET, E.C.

1877.

LONDON :
BRADBURY, AGNEW, & CO., PRINTERS, WHITEFRIARS.

PREFACE.

N publishing this work, it is not my wish or intention to attempt to teach the Player how to use, the Maker how to build, or the Architect how to encase, the second instrument mentioned in the Bible, but to put before the descendants of Jubal that which may incite them to continue to improve the noble instrument, which the combined efforts of taste, science, and skill, have brought to its present degree of excellence.

JOHN NORBURY.

32, Gordon Square, London,
April, 1877.

CONTENTS.

CHAPTER I.

CHAPTER II.

CHAPTER III.

CHAPTER IV.

CHAPTER V.

CONTENTS.

ILLUSTRATIONS.

—◄◦►◄◦►—

ILLUSTRATIONS.

INDEX TO NOTES ON ORGANS.

THE BOX OF WHISTLES.

CHAPTER I.

INTRODUCTORY.

HE Box of Whistles! what a quaint title! Yes, but a good one, I think, for this book, as the old organ of Father Smith's in St. Paul's, "The Box of Whistles," as Sir Christopher Wren contemptuously called it, was the first organ I ever saw, and which gave me my bent in the liking of things pertaining to the organ. Well do I recollect standing, a very small boy, under the Dome of St. Paul's, on a dark winter's afternoon, looking at Grinling Gibbons' noble case, hearing some grand out-going voluntary, and trying to see the angels put their trumpets to their mouths, when the reeds were drawn, which I could never catch them doing. Now the organ is perhaps the only instrument which gives equal gratification to three separate classes of individuals, who are often very different in other respects, the Musician, the Mechanician, and the Architect. The Musician likes it for its tone and power, giving sounds which no other instrument can give, and imitating the tones of almost every other instrument. The Mechanician likes it as a complicated machine ; and the different modes of its action, and the varied ways of supplying it with wind, are sources of pleasure and amusement to him. The Architect admires its noble look, as it stands towering high in Cathedral, Church, or Concert Room, its case covered with carved work, and its pipes bright with gilding, be its style Gothic or Renaissance. Remember that an organ is built, other musical instruments are made. The Musician very likely cares not for its look, so long as the tone pleases him, and possibly knows little, and cares less, how the sound is produced. The Mechanician is pleased to know how and why certain tones and effects are obtained, caring perhaps very little for real music, and as for the case, he never gives it a thought. The Architect may have but small knowledge of music ; as for the mechanical part of the instrument, it is not in the least in his line ; but he does feel the impress of its grandeur, and admires the complex design of a large and well-built organ case. I am no player, but I much like the sound of an organ, and to hear good music played on it.

Of mechanics I have some knowledge, but it is in general difficult to get a sight of the internal works of an organ. They are well described in Hopkins's work, "The Organ," 1870, and the "Encyclopédie Roret," 1849, which, in its valuable reprint of Dom Bedos, "L'Art du Facteur des Orgues," gives excellent details and good engravings. To me it seems a pity that this work has not been translated into English, and brought down to the present time, as technical terms in a foreign language are difficult even to good linguists. To the organ builder, it is a more useful work than that of Mr. Hopkins, as the French book is for the practical man, while the English work is for the general reader. I am not an architect, but in my leisure hours architecture and drawing have been

B

my amusements. For some years I have sketched and taken notes of the different organs which I have had the good fortune to see either at home or abroad, and I now venture to publish (a small quota to general knowledge) my notes and drawings of organs, the collecting of which has been my recreation for many an hour. I think that the ground on which I now venture has not as yet been occupied by any one.

Mr. Hopkins gives but general information about organ cases, and no engravings. The "Encyclopédie Roret" gives more particulars, and also furnishes a few engravings, and the English edition of "Seidel's Treatise on the Organ" is very cursory on this subject. Further information can be gleaned from the Rev. F. H. Sutton's "Short Account of Organs Built in England," &c., 1847, which gives small woodcuts of the typical cases of the old English builders, and at the end of the work, five designs of the late Mr. Pugin are given, which are worth studying; and from "Some Account of the Mediæval Organ Case," &c., 1866, and "Church Organs," 1872, by the Rev. F. H. Sutton, both of which are very good for reference. Mr. Faulkner's "Designs for Organs," 1838, is now rather out of date, but C. K. K. Bishop's "Notes on Church Organs" gives nice suggestive plates. If the very fine and exhaustive work on "Foreign Gothic Organs," mentioned by the Rev. Mr. Sutton in his "Mediæval Organ Case," 1866, should ever see light, it would be first-class, as it would contain drawings and details of the best Gothic organs, which are rare, and of which it is difficult to obtain drawings or descriptions. There are many small works which give drawings, &c., to which I do not more particularly refer, out of which useful information may be gleaned.

What I wish to put before my readers in this book, is a short description of the different classes of organ cases, with my remarks and notes of various instruments, illustrated by lithographs and chromo-lithographs, from my own sketches. Having now explained my intention, I have to beg those who read this, my first work, not to be very severe on my errors and shortcomings.

CHAPTER II.

THE ORGAN CASE.

(BUFFET, *French*; ORGEL GEHÄUSE, *German*; KIST o' WHISTLES, *Scotticè*).

Division into Four Classes.—Subdivisions of ditto.

ORGAN cases may broadly be divided into four classes. Firstly, those which stand at the end of the nave or transept of a Church, or the end of a Concert Room. Secondly, organs which are pendent from the side of the nave or choir of a large Church. Thirdly, organs which stand on Choir Screens; and Fourthly, organs standing on the ground. Of these classes many sub-divisions may be made. Of the organs in these four classes, those in No. 1 are in general the most imposing, those in No. 2 the most picturesque, those in No. 3 the best for sound, and those in No. 4 require some skill to make them rival their compeers. Class 1 may be sub-divided into—

A. Those which fill the entire end, or nearly so, of the building in which they stand;

B. Those which have a window, or "Rose" over them; and,

C. Divided Organs, and those with exceptionally designed cases.

A. This sub-class (a very ordinary one in England and Holland) has the finest cases in the world, for I suppose that the grandest and most elaborate case in Europe is that in St. Jan's Church, Hertogenbosch (Bois-le-Duc), rich in sculptured oak, and bright with burnished tin pipes and gilding. Externally, although it has not got so many stops, it is as large as its well-known neighbour at Haarlem, which has till lately been considered the type of a "Great Organ." Haarlem has a noble case, with excellent pipe-work within, but its effect is injured by paint. The organ in the Hof Kirche, Lucerne, also has quaint oak carving in its thirty-two feet front, and for pretty cases, that at St. Jacques, Liége, by some considered the best of its kind, and the Organs in St. Lawrence, Jewry, and St. Stephen's, Walbrook, the last looking somewhat like a miniature of that at Troyes, may be cited as good examples.

B. A sub-class to which very many of the large French organs may be referred. In general, these are more picturesque than those in Sub-class A, not that the absolute design is so, but that the architectural effect of the window above the case makes a most effective combination. In France, the usual window is a Rose, a form I think the best for the termination of a nave or transept, and when this is filled with stained glass, as is often the case, the effect is all that can be desired. The organs in Amiens, Rheims, Troyes, and Rouen Cathedrals, and also in Rouen in the Churches of St. Ouen and St. Maclou, are first-class examples. This sub-class is rare in England, few of our churches being sufficiently lofty to allow an organ to stand in such a position.

Sub-class *C.* is employed to show the west window. Fair examples are to be seen at St. Gudule, Bruxelles, and in Gray's Inn Chapel. Among the exceptional cases, that in the Cathedral Church of St. Vitus at Prague, is one of the most curious, being cut up into four divisions, and scattered about the west galleries ; and for an ugly style of exceptional case, there is one in a church in Ghent, about as ugly as can well be wished.

Class II. This class, as I have mentioned before, is highly picturesque, but is not very common. Good examples are to be seen in Strasburg and Chartres Cathedrals, and in the Minster at Freiburg, in Bresgau, all pendent in the nave ; and there is a grand modern example hanging in the north side of the Choir at Ely. Organs which may be placed in this class are not uncommonly built against the east wall of the Transept in large Belgian churches : one in the cathedral church of St. Bavon, Ghent, is a good example. There must be some difficulty in building a large instrument in this position, and a lofty church is required to contain it.

Class III. may likewise be subdivided into two divisions : *A.* Single Cases, often with a Choir Organ in front ; and *B.* Divided Cases. Of the former sub-class, the old organ in St. Paul's was in every way a fine example. The old organ in Durham Cathedral was the best of Father Smith's usual design, all his cases having a strong family likeness, that at St. Paul's being almost the only exception. The case on the Grand Screen in York Minster, although perhaps not in the best taste, is effective ; and of the latter sub-class, the organ in St. Jacques, Antwerp, is excellent, and is worth the study of any one who may have to erect a divided "Screen Organ." The much-divided organ case in Westminster Abbey I am Goth enough to call bad.

Class IV. The divisions of this class are numerous, and often occur in modern churches. *A.*, those standing on the floor against the wall of the nave or chancel. St. Mary's, Nottingham, has a first-class modern specimen, an amplification of the organ case in Strasburg Cathedral. *B.* Those standing in the nave, aisle, or some corner. A good example of an old case in the first position, is in St. Clement's, East Cheap ; and the organ in All Hallows, Lombard Street, is a good specimen of one in the second position. Both these instruments, not so many years ago, stood in galleries at the west end of their respective churches. *C.* Those in Organ Chambers, examples of which, I am sorry to say, are common in new and restored Churches. *D.* Those in Organ Chapels, which are rather better for effect than those in Sub-class *C.* St. George's, Doncaster, is an example of an organ of the largest size in this position. *E.* Those standing free under the arches of the Choir of a Cathedral or large church. In the Cathedral at Hereford is a large modern organ in this position. *F.* Organs with Divided cases. St. Paul's and Durham Cathedral have good examples of this form, which I fancy is modern and peculiar to England.

In Italy and Spain, there are often two Great organs, one on each side of the Choir or Nave, which arrangement, conjointly with a double Choir of Singers, is capable of the grandest effects of antiphonal music. As good examples in Italy, may be mentioned the organs in Milan Cathedral on each side of the Choir, and those in Como Cathedral on each side of the Nave. Those in Milan are externally alike, and those in Como differ in appearance. In Spain, two organs are usual in Cathedrals and large churches, and the two organs in Seville Cathedral have magnificent cases.

Class I.—*A.* Filling the entire end of the building.	Class IV.—*A.* Against wall of nave or choir.
B. With a window or rose over.	*B.* Standing in a corner, or in aisle of nave.
C. Divided and exceptional cases.	*C.* In organ chambers.
,, II.—No subdivision.	*D.* In organ chapels.
,, III.—*A.* Single cases, or with choir in front.	*E.* Under arches of choir.
B. Divided cases.	*F.* Divided instruments.

CHAPTER III.

WHAT A GOOD CASE SHOULD BE.

Style not necessarily Gothic.—Renaissance Style.—Tin Pipes now seldom used.—An Organ Case need not correspond with the Style of Architecture of the Building.—English Cases during the last hundred years.—An Organ Case should be good.—Unequal Number of Towers.—Ponts.—Oak and other Woods.—Culs-de-Lampe.—Ornaments.—Arrangement of Pipes.—Arrangement of Towers.

EFORE I proceed any further with this Chapter, I may as well mention that I fear I may a little shock some persons with my views of what is a good organ case. I have long ceased to think that nothing but Gothic is correct, and feel pleasure in looking at any style of architecture (excepting the modern ultra-Gothic, and even this affords me a certain amount of amusement). I have, when the Gothic fit was upon me, passed many a fine organ with a mere glance, at which I should now look with delight. When I see some of our modern Norman and Gothic cases, I wonder what the men of the date which these make-believe cases pretend to be would think of them. I suspect that they would look at them with amazement. The illuminations in manuscripts do not give us much help, and the drawings which they hand down to us are those of very small instruments. Some few cases in the later period of Gothic are in existence at Perpignan, Strasburg, Gonesse, New Radnor, and in some few places in Germany, but with the exception of the one at Strasburg, I have not been so fortunate as to get a sight of any. With the advent of the Renaissance Style, organs began to increase in size, so that larger and more architectural cases were requisite, and we do not even now excel in design and workmanship many of the old Flemish, Dutch, and French organs. Carved oak is now an expensive luxury, and pipes of tin, with their silver-like lustre, are things of the past. The price of tin, and the cheap contract system, have a good deal to do with this state of things; and town atmosphere seems to tarnish tin work in a very short time: about Manchester it cannot be used, and at Rouen I have seen bright pipe-work, which had been up but a few years, look as tarnished as if it had been up for fifty years at least. I like an organ to have a really good case; it is a large and necessary piece of furniture in both church and concert-room; and I can see no reason why it should not be in keeping with the building in which it stands. By this I do not intend that its architectural style should be the same, but that there should be a certain agreement together, and a fitness one for the other. Viollet le Duc, I think, was wise in retaining the old Renaissance case of the organ in Notre Dame (Paris), when the whole of its contents were taken away, and an entirely new organ erected in it. No man in France could have better designed a Gothic case, but he preferred leaving the old work, which well suited its position. In general all fittings of a later date than the building in which they stand, if they are really good of their kind, should be respected. Much new work, intended to be quite in keeping with the building, and following precedent, is but little more than guesswork. In an old Norman church, it would be I think foolish to erect a Norman case: we have nothing to guide us as to what an organ was like in outward appearance at that date, but we do know that it was a rather rudely made affair, from "Theophilus's Treatise on Organ Building;" and we are equally at sea for any precedent for an early Gothic organ. Late cases are here and there to be seen, and many of them are handsome, but it was the builders of the Renaissance Period who first erected those structures of carved wood, for the abode of the noblest of instruments. For many years good cases continued to be built; they never quite ceased erecting them in France and Belgium; but I have nothing to say in favour of our English cases for the last hundred years. We do better now, but I look upon caseless organs, with their rows of painted pipes, as something horrid. A good piano always has a good case; we do not dream of buying, or the vendor of selling, a first-class instrument in a paltry one; and why a really well-built and good-toned organ is put into a plain deal varnished case, like a common cheap schoolroom piano, is a puzzle to me. Father Smith appears to have had a pattern case, which is excellent in outline, and suitable to all his organs, large or small, except his chamber instruments, and Harris also rarely departed from his one design, a very pretty one. The old French builders appeared to have followed a few general rules, viz., that an organ should have an unequal number of towers, say three, five, or seven; and if, as was usual, the Choir case stood in front, it should have a smaller number of towers, say the Great case had five, the Choir had three; that if the centre tower of the Great was the tallest, the centre tower of the Choir should be the least, and *vice versâ;* and very good rules these are. It was also their practice to form the mouths of the pipes in the towers, different to those in the flats, and the pipes in the towers stood on square blocks of wood (ponts), whilst the pipes in the flats stood on plinths. These little niceties add much to the appearance of an organ. Renatus Harris used to finish his pipes in the French manner. I prefer oak to any wood for case work. Polished ebonised wood with ormolu mouldings (as at the Foundling) looks well, and good cabinet work has been done in mahogany. Walnut and rosewood may do for chamber instruments, but would have rather a harmonium look about them. If I were building a drawing-room organ, I should certainly use oak, with plenty of carving and no varnish; wax polish would perhaps be advisable to tone down the new look, but with very fine sharp work the wood should be left as it comes fresh from the carver's hands. In a cheap instrument plain deal with good varnish looks better than painted wood, with or without stencilled patterns, and where the large wood pipes are shown, they are best plain. The upper part of the case being wider than the base (a very common arrange-ment in old French instruments), is an improvement to its outline. Another French usage, to support the large outer towers on giants, is good, especially for their large cases; and " the culs-de-lampe," or consoles of the towers, are improved by sculptured heads, paniers of flowers, or intricate open-work. I do not object to what I have heard called a "covey" of plump cherubim. With respect to the mouldings, a little departure from strict rules does not hurt, and it is best not to err on the side of shallowness: bold projections and deep curves look well, and circular towers should project rather more than half their diameter; the cornices should certainly project boldly—recollect they are wood, and rules for stone cornices need not be closely adhered to, but they must not overhang each other (Chevaucher is the French term), as that does not look well. Statues on the summits of the towers I like to see, although of course they are a useless expense; and there is a wide choice as to what they should be. Angels with trumpets or harps are excellent. King David with his harp, St. Cecilia with her organ, are very usual. Winged angels with lutes are not uncommon on Flemish organs: the patron saint of the church is correct. Pope Gregory, as the founder of the Catholic chant; St. Ambrose, the writer of the "Te Deum;" Guido D'Arezzo, the inventor of the gamut, and several others may be mentioned as fit subjects for statuary work. Crowns and mitres for Church and State are good terminals for an English organ, and the arms of the reigning sovereign can well be introduced in the carving: for a good example, see the old organ in St. Paul's. The shades (claires voies) of an organ should be well carved, and in some designs the introduction of winged angel heads is very suitable: in general they should be left plain; gilding clashes with bright tin, and offers no contrast with gilt pipes. In the north of Europe the tops of the pipes are concealed by the shades, but in Italy they are free, and it is an open question which mode is the best. Either of these arrangements is better than the tops of the pipes shewing above the case with fanciful crowns on them. The northern mode saves a little in height, which sometimes is an advantage. Carved open-work or wings at the sides of the organ, though useless, are often picturesque; occasionally they hide large wood pipes posted outside the case, which are, in general, additions to the original contents, and then they are useful.

For effect, the wood-work should not fill the entire breadth of the space in which the organ stands, but shew itself as a case, and not as a screen to hide the internal arrangements. The case at Lucerne, good as the work is, fails in this particular: it is a screen at the west end of the church, to hide the organ, not a case for it. English organs often err in the reverse manner, and look like square boxes. A broader and shallower form is preferable, but English feeling is, I am afraid, in favour of the square form. The case at Haarlem has been quoted as spoiling the tone of the instrument, and on the other hand, a French writer on the organ, C. M. Philbert, states, "Un artiste habitant Paris nous disait, ces jours derniers, qu'en payant le prix fixé pour les auditions particulières de l'orgue de Haarlem, on ne payait pas trop cher, né fût-ce que le seul plaisir d'en admirer la magnificence extérieure." I tried at Haarlem to detect if the tone were smothered by the case, but could not in the least perceive any such defect. The quality is very mellow, which is very pleasing to the ear, and is without the harshness which now-a-days is called boldness of tone. Towers boldly projecting, either half circular or pointed, are an improvement to the design of a case. Flat towers, which in general are flush with the flats, or only project slightly, although used in some few cases, do not give that play of light and shade which is so effective in a design. Where shutters, curtains, or blinds, are used, projecting towers are in the way; but in Holland are to be seen small cases with shutters, which follow all the ins-and-outs of cases much broken in plan. They must be difficult to make and to keep from warping, and when large must be troublesome to open or close. Opinions are divided as to the usefulness of these appendages to an organ, no doubt they are often most picturesque.

CHAPTER IV.

THE ARRANGEMENT OF THE PIPES.

Number of the Pipes.—Not all of the Same Height.—Two Tiers of Pipes.—Oval and Circular Openings.—Pipes arranged in Perspective.—Carved Panels.—Inverted Pipes.—Double Pipes.—Projecting Mouths.—Fancy Mouldings on Pipes.—Pipes, gilt—diapered—painted—tin—bronzed.—Tubes of Reed Stops projecting horizontally.—Tuba at York.

 HE usual number of pipes in each tower is in England three, in France five, and in Germany seven (in the Tyrol, flat towers with seven pipes are the rule); but to these numbers there are many exceptions. Towers with two stories of pipes are in use in Holland, Belgium, and Germany, but I cannot call to mind any in England or in France. In general the number of pipes in the upper story exceeds that of the lower. A single pipe either forming a compartment, or projecting so as to form a tower, is not a good feature, except when, as in some of the North German organs, a thirty-two feet pipe is used as a tower. In some flat towers, four pipes are inserted instead of five; but an uneven number, I think, is more satisfactory to the eye. It does not look well for all the pipes in a compartment to be of the same height, and it is still worse when all the flats are alike : for this reason the organ in Exeter Hall is ugly, and good as the case is in Rouen Cathedral, it would be much improved if some gradation in the pipe lengths were introduced into its four similar compartments.

In the flats, two tiers of pipes are common in English and Dutch organs, and in Holland more often appear in large cases. Oval and circular openings for pipes are used in England, and more rarely in France : it is an artificial mode of arranging pipe work. There are a few examples of pipes being arranged to form a perspective, which may be looked upon as a fanciful conceit. Panels carved to give the same effect are not quite so *outré*. In Holland and North Germany, inverted pipes are to be met with : they in general stand on the wood framing, but at Perpignan (France) there is a flat of inverted pipes which hang from the case by their feet. I fancy that in general these are shams, but an inverted pipe would not be liable to be choked with dust. In Dutch fronts occasionally double pipes, or what may be more correctly styled two pipes with their feet joined together, are used : those that I have seen were dummies, as no means of supplying them with wind was to be seen. Projecting mouths are a great finish to large pipes. French builders are often very good at this work ; but it may be overdone, as in the new organ in Chester Cathedral, where the mouths are certainly exaggerated. Old French builders sometimes inserted a few pipes with various fancy mouldings about them, brightened with paint. The organ of Gonesse has some, and two are preserved as curiosities in the Museum at Beauvais. Pipes with their surface hammered into facets are rare. At Hertogenbosch, the centre pipes of the towers are so treated, and are also plain gilt ; but that in the central tower is parcel gilt. Belgian and Dutch organs often have the mouths of their bright tin pipes gilt, which has a good effect. I have no great liking for diapered (painted or illuminated) pipes, even if it has taken a fortnight to paint each, as has lately been done ; it gives the idea that it is necessary to hide bad workmanship, or poor metal. Coronals to the pipes, however elaborate, had best be eschewed, although in caseless organs they give a sort of finish to the pipes. But after all I have said against painted pipes, one cannot help liking the bright appearance of a small case, with well-coloured pipes, even if one doubts how it will look after a few years, when the freshness has departed. Plain gilding perhaps looks well longer than anything else.

Tin pipes, when dull, have a very neglected look ; and nothing can look worse than bronzed pipes. In Spain, it is the custom to place the Reed Stops so that their tubes project horizontally, or at an angle from the case : this throws out their sound.* This arrangement is not common in England, but might be adopted with good effect both for tone and appearance. The Tuba at York, projecting from the west façade of the organ, is most satisfactory in both respects; any arranging of trumpets, like a fan or half-circle at the top of the case, is as well avoided.

CHAPTER V.

THE CHOIR ORGAN AS A SEPARATE CASE.

As a Screen to the Player.—Choir Front in the Lower Part of Case.

 I.THOUGH organs now do not consist merely of a Great and Choir (or Chair) organ, the two cases add much to the look of an instrument, and the Choir case makes an excellent screen to conceal the organist. Old organs of any pretensions are rarely without it, and for church organs, which stand in a gallery, or in any other raised position, it should always make its appearance. For a concert-room organ, or an organ standing on the ground, it is not required. In some German instruments, the Choir case is so small, that one suspects that it is a sham, or at most merely a console to hold the keys. In France, reversed key-boards are coming into fashion ; and to hide them, a screen of pipes is a pardonable deception. A German custom of putting the Choir Front into the lower part of the case of the Great Organ, under its pipes, where the key-board is usually placed, has a very uncomfortable look ; although we know that Great and Choir pipes are often put into the same case, and there is no reason why, if this is done, the exterior of the case should not show it. Still there is something strange in the appearance.

CHAPTER VI.

THE MINOR DETAILS OF AN ORGAN.

Room in the Loft.—Loft should not be used as a Singing Gallery.—Reversed Key-boards.—Black Keys for Naturals, &c.—Rows of Stops, perpendicular, horizontal.—Varied Forms of Pedals.—Music Desk.—Lights.—Looking Glass.—Clock.—Carving between the Pipes.—Fox-tail Stop.—Electric and Pneumatic Actions.

 T is a pity that many small things about an organ are not a little more cared for. The cramped room in the loft is uncomfortable for the player; he is often jammed between the two cases, or his back touches the balustrade of the gallery, rendering it a matter of difficulty for any one who may be in the loft with him, to get from one side of the instrument to the other, which is troublesome if the player requires assistance, as is sometimes wanted ; and a loft should have comfortable sitting and kneeling accommodation : an organist and those with him in the loft ought to have the means of following the service, and hearing

---

* At Leeds, the pipes of the solo portion of the Town-hall Organ are entirely placed horizontally, and it is stated that this increases their power from 20 to 30 per cent.

the sermon, with a certain amount of ease. The organ-loft being used as a singing-gallery is to be avoided, except when it is a spacious gallery, and even then the organist should have plenty of elbow room, and be screened off more or less from the singers. A reversed key-board rather complicates the mechanism, and therefore should be avoided, as the supposed advantage of the player being able to see what is being done in the church is problematical, for with his music before him, it is next to impossible for him to do so. The organist at Exeter Hall used to face the conductor, but some years back the key-board was re-arranged in its usual position. The organist's place between the Great and Choir of Father Smith's organ at Durham, when it stood on the north side of the Choir, was as good as could be wished. Black keys for naturals, and white (ivory) for the sharps look well : they are sometimes to be seen in old instruments, and should be retained ; the contrast between them and more modern key-boards, which have a strong harmonium or American organ look, is in their favour. Every player has his own views as to whether the old perpendicular rows of stop-handles, or the French horizontal rows, are the best, and no one form of pedals, plain, concave, radiating, or both concave and radiating, gives universal satisfaction. A good music-desk should be fixed to every organ : in general they are ricketty things, and will only hold a little octavo hymn-tune book. The lights, be they candles or gas, should be securely fixed, and not liable to be knocked against by the player.

A looking-glass, which should be a part of the organ, and not a shaving-glass hung up with string and nails, should be fixed so that the player can see down the church ; and something better than fastening with a pin to the side of the desk a shabby bit of paper with the list of music, &c., might be arranged. In England, Holland, and Normandy, a clock is occasionally part of the organ case, sometimes on the Great, and sometimes on the Choir case, and it is a useful accessory. Sometimes when there is no Choir Organ, it is inserted in the front of the gallery. In Whitehall Chapel a clock hangs from the ceiling under the organ-loft, a puzzle how any one can get at it to wind it up. In some few organs carved wood-work is introduced between the feet of the pipes, so as to fill up the triangular space. The pipes in the towers of St. Lawrence, Jewry, have a sort of tall leaf between them. From a French work I give the following extract : " A la tribune de l'orgue de la Cathédral de Barcelonne, on voit une tête de Maure suspendue par son turban. Lorsque les jeux les plus doux se font entendre, la figure frémit ; mais si les sons augmentent de force, ses yeux roulent dans leurs orbites, ses dents s'entre-choquent, et toute la face est en proie à d'horribles convulsions. Le mécanisme qui produisait ces effets a été supprimé." This must be the delight or horror of small children, and no one would dream of such an addition to a modern church or concert-room organ, neither would the fox-tail stop be inserted, although a person who was fond of "curios" might put them into a chamber instrument. I do not make more than the passing remark on the electric and pneumatic actions, that they are very valuable adjuncts to a large instrument, and afford great facilities in many ways to the player, as they are well explained and illustrated in the last (1870) edition of Hopkins's "Organ."

NOTES ON ORGANS AT HOME AND ABROAD.

NOTES ON ENGLISH ORGANS.

LTHOUGH English cases cannot in general, in size and carving, compete with their compeers on the continent, many of them are very good, and might be studied by modern architects and builders. The contents of our old instruments are less than those of the same date in France, Germany, and Holland, and the Pedal Organ was for many years neglected. Our modern organs now can vie with any; and if their cases were better, they could hold their own against their foreign rivals. There are some good modern cases, but they are the exception and not the rule.

I now give my notes, which from time to time I have made, of our English instruments.

LONDON.

FATHER SMITH'S ORGAN IN ST. PAUL'S.—This instrument, when it stood where it was originally intended to be, on the Choir Screen, both looked and sounded well. The case, which was a very exceptional one for Father Smith, who hardly ever varied from his four-tower arrangement, had fine carving by Grinling Gibbons, and, with the Choir Organ in front, harmonised well with the handsome oak Stalls. Some years ago it was pulled down and put over the Stalls on the north side of the Choir, where, to my taste, it did not look or sound well, and the Choir case was placed in front of the large transept organ, where it looked small and out of place. The old case is now divided, and placed on each side of the Choir, the old Choir case put in its proper position, before one half of the Great case, and a new Choir case of similar design made to complete the other. The contents are by Willis, and it is a good specimen of a modern cathedral organ.

ALL HALLOWS, LOMBARD STREET.—A pretty case of peculiar design, which used to stand in the gallery at the west end of the Church, but is now placed on the floor in the south-east corner. The case consists of two towers, one on each side of the instrument, with a circular opening between them, filled with pipe-work, above which stands a small tower, with a flat of pipes on each side. There is a quaintness about it which I like.

CHRIST CHURCH, NEWGATE STREET.—Has a large fine organ standing at the west end of the Church; its four towers, surmounted by mitres and crowns, give it a Church and State look. Although the case is large, there is nothing very striking about it; but the quality of its contents is good.

ST. CLEMENT'S, EASTCHEAP.—The organ stands on the south side of the Church; it formerly stood at the west end, and is very similar to that at All Hallows, but of a more elaborate design, consisting of two large towers, between which is an oval of pipes, upon which stands a small tower, with an oval of pipes on each side, above which stand two small flats of pipes. Modern taste has heavily painted the pipes; in fact, I never saw so much solid paint put on metal pipes; and in my opinion when they were plain gilt they looked much better.

ST. LAWRENCE, JEWRY.—The organ, which stands at the west end of the Church, has as fine and as correctly designed a case as can well be. The carving is excellent, and the old

ST LAWRENCE JEWRY

3RD DEC.R 1870

ST MAGNUS THE MARTYR, LONDON BRIDGE

MAY 1871

S‍ᵗ SEPULCHRE — SNOW HILL.

10ᵗʰ MAY 1871.

French rules for designing an organ case have been carried out with the best effect. Since I sketched it, a new inside has been put into it, and the case enlarged in very good taste. It is now, perhaps, to be critical, a little too square in form, but it ranks among the best in London.

ST. MAGNUS THE MARTYR, LONDON BRIDGE.—This organ, remarkable as the first which had a swell, is rather peculiar in design. The dark wood carving is good, and there is a quiet look of solid workmanship about the case which is much to be commended.

ST. OLAVE'S, SOUTHWARK.—The organ, with four towers, and famous for having a thirty-two feet stop on the Great Organ, after the manner of large German instruments, stands at the west end, in a good plain case, but one that would hardly be worth adopting as a model for another instrument.

ST. SEPULCHRE'S has a handsome large organ, with a Choir case in front. The wood-work is fine, the mouths of the pipes nicely shaped, and the effect of the angular tower in the centre good. The case, I should think, must have looked better before the two wings of large pipes were added.

CHESTER CATHEDRAL.

The new organ, erected in 1876, stands in a stone loft, with marble pillars, under the north arch of the centre tower. It has an abundance of carved Gothic wood-work, and the pipes are plain gilt. The mouths of the large pipes are shaped in the French style, but appear to me a little exaggerated. On the Choir Screen stands the Echo Organ, which puts me in mind of that in Notre-Dame de Bruges, on a very small scale. The thirty-two feet pedal pipes (wood) stand on the ground at the end of the north transept. They were incomplete when I saw them in November, 1876, and I should very much doubt if they will prove effective. Water-power and a gas-engine have been tried for blowing, and did not succeed, and a steam-engine was being erected.

DURHAM CATHEDRAL.

A fine organ of Father Smith's usual pattern formerly stood, with its Choir Organ in front, on the Choir Screen. Some years ago it was removed and placed on the north side of the Choir; and, in 1876, has given place to a new divided organ, by Willis, half standing on each side of the Choir. The arrangements of the old organ loft were very comfortable; I mention this, as but too often the loft is so cramped and inconvenient that the player can never be quite at ease.

YORK MINSTER.

One of our largest cathedral organs stands on the magnificent Choir Screen. It is a huge, square mass of painted pipes and Gothic carving. The most picturesque part of the instrument is the tuba, the pipes of which are arranged horizontally, pointing down the nave. This stop is the best of its kind I know.

This is but a meagre account of English organs, as it only includes those which I have had the means of studying: I ought to have written about the Temple organ, that in Westminster Abbey, the huge instrument in the Albert Hall, and the one in the Crystal Palace. That in the Temple has been described, much better than I can do it, by Edmund Macrory, in his "Few Notes on the Temple Organ." I hope that some day the Abbey authorities will see how poor, not in tone, but in appearance, their present organ is. They have ample space to erect a magnificent case. The Albert Hall organ is an attempt at a new style of case, which I think is a failure; and the Handel organ has a very ordinary (except for its size) façade, with four towers, and the usual painted pipes.

NOTES ON FRENCH ORGANS.

ABBEVILLE.

 *T. WOLFRAM.*—A fine organ stands in a gallery which fills the first compartment of the nave, so that the case stands well away from the west window. The great case has five towers, of five pipes each, the smallest in the centre, on the top of which is a winged angel, with a sword in one hand and a scroll in the other: On each side is a flat of five pipes, then a middling-sized tower, beyond these are flats of four pipes each, and then two great towers, which overhang the sides of the case. The Choir Organ, which stands in front, consists of two flats, of ten pipes each, and three towers, the largest in the centre, each containing seven pipes. The Accompaniment Organ (by this term I mean an organ standing in the Choir, to accompany the Priests' voices) stands on the north side of the Choir, in a plain modern flat-topped case, with a little Gothic work about it. It is played from a reverse key-board in the Stalls. Tone fair. 1875.

ST. SEPULCHRE.—The west-end organ has a plain classic face of oak, with three towers, the tallest in the middle. The Choir Organ in front has three towers, disposed in the same manner. In a Chapel, on the south-east side of the Church, is a modern Gothic organ, the front of which forms a sort of reredos to an Altar, an arrangement certainly not to be commended. 1875.

AMIENS.

THE CATHEDRAL.—The Great Organ, which stands in a gallery at the west end of the Church, is one of the oldest in France. It is simple in design, consisting of three flat towers, with flats between them. The case is painted blue, and much gilded. It has a Choir Organ in front, which is an addition, and rather Belgian in style. It is a good-sized instrument, but does not look large enough for so spacious a Church.

In the north aisle of the Choir is an Accompaniment Organ, in a common case, with no pipes ; air-holes are cut in the wood-work, some of which show through the backs of the Stalls, from which it is played. The tone of the Great Organ flue stops is coarse, but that of the reeds good, and on the whole the instrument is very suitable for the large Cathedral in which it stands. The quality of the Accompaniment Organ is very fair. In 1868 I heard them both played at Mass. The players were good, especially the organist of the large instrument. 1868, 1875.

ST. ———.—In a Church, the name of which I omitted to note, was an organ, the front of which consisted of a painting of an organ front (scene-painter's work). It looked dirty, as if it had been up for some time. I suppose they were either short of funds to carry out the design, or there was some yet unsettled dispute pending ; such things happen nearer home than Amiens. 1868.

BAYEUX.

THE CATHEDRAL.—The large organ stands at the west end of the Church, with its Choir in front. It stands in a gallery, supported by a stone arch thrown across the nave. The great case consists of a large central tower with five pipes, surmounted by an urn, on each side of which is a flat of seven pipes, then a small tower, containing one pipe only ; again a flat of seven pipes, and at each end of the case is a tower containing three pipes, which are supported by figures. The

St WOLFRAM ABBEVILLE

14TH MAY, 1875.

ST ETIENNE—BEAUVAIS

18TH MAY. 1875.

Choir Organ consists of a small tower of five pipes in the centre, with a flat on each side, and beyond them a taller tower of three pipes. The tone is full, but wanting in sweetness, and is deficient in bass. Under the arch, on the north side of the Choir, next the centre tower, is an Accompaniment Organ, in a very handsome case with three towers, and of fair quality in tone. About this district, most of the organs stand on an arch, thrown across the west end of the nave. 1866.

BEAUVAIS.

THE CATHEDRAL.—The Great Organ stands in an exceptional position, at the south end of the east aisle of the south transept, standing as forward as the first column of the transept, leaving space between it and the end of the transept, for bellows, &c. Although one of the largest organs in France, the case is plain and simple, consisting merely of three towers of five pipes each, the smallest in the centre, with flats between, and a Choir Organ in front, consisting of a long flat, with two circular towers. Above the Great Organ case, stands some old painted screen-work. As far as the case is concerned, the organ is not worthy of the lofty Cathedral in which it stands. I did not hear this organ, so cannot judge of its tone. In the Choir is a modern Gothic organ, with three gabled flats, and in the north transept is a harmonium. 1875.

ST. ETIENNE has, at the west end, a good-sized organ of dark oak, standing in a gallery, supported by two square oak pillars. The Great Organ case consists of three towers, with five pipes each. The largest, which are at each end, are supported by angels, and crowned with vases, and the centre tower is surmounted by an angel. The flats between the towers are each divided in half by a pilaster. The Choir Organ, also in dark oak, has three towers, the least in the centre. In the spaces between the Great Organ case and the sides of the nave, are wooden arches filled in with lattice-work, behind which is placed a quantity of pipe-work, so that the organ is really larger than it appears to be at first sight. 1875.*

BOULOGNE.

THE CATHEDRAL.—Over the west door stands a large modern organ, consisting simply of panels of open work, and without any pipes showing. 1875.

CAEN.

ST. ETIENNE.—At the west end is a large organ, with four towers; those at the side of the case are borne by giants. In front stands the Choir Organ, consisting of two flats, and three towers of five pipes each, the least in the centre. Under the north arch of the centre tower (the Choir reaching as far as the western piers of the same) is an Accompaniment Organ of modern Gothic work. In the middle of the Choir is a harmonium, which I was told was for the boys. 1866.

ST. JEAN has a handsome organ, with its Choir Organ in front. It also shows, under the arch against which it stands, a little front facing the west entrance. 1866.

ST. PIERRE—At the west end stands a large old organ, with its Choir in front, as usual, and on the south side of the Choir is a small Accompaniment Organ. 1866.

ST. TRINITÉ.—In the north transept stands a shabby-looking organ. This handsome Norman church should have something more worthy of it. 1866.

* In the Museum at Beauvais are two curious organ pipes, with raised mouldings and painted decorations, which I believe are some of the original pipes of the old organ at Gonesse.

COUTANCES.

THE CATHEDRAL.—At the west end of the church, supported by four pillars, arranged two and two on each side, stands a fine organ with the customary Choir in front. Among the sketches of David Roberts, which were sold after his death, was a very good one of this instrument. Under the north arch of the centre tower, stands a small modern Gothic Accompaniment Organ, consisting of four panels with flat tops. It is played from the front row of the Choir Stalls, the Choir, as at Caen, extending as far as the western arch of the centre tower. 1866.

ST. NICOLAS.—At the west end stands an old organ in a very English-looking case, with three towers, the largest of which is in the centre. As the case is flush with the front of the gallery, the key-board must be either at the back, or on one side of the instrument. 1866.

ST. PIERRE.—In a gallery, standing across the western bay of the nave, unsupported by pillar or arch, stands the organ with its Choir in front, in a very ordinary case. 1866.

DIEPPE.

ST. JACQUES.—Supported on wooden pillars at the west end of the church, is a large early Renaissance organ, with a Choir in front, in a dirty condition. 1866.

ST. RÉMI has an organ very similar to St. Jacques, not quite so old, which, when I saw it, was in a very shabby state.

DIJON.

THE CATHEDRAL.—The organ is in a Grand case at the west end. By some people it is considered one of the finest cases in France. I have never been able to get a drawing or photograph of it, and omitted to sketch it myself. 1855.

LAON.

THE CATHEDRAL.—At the end of the north transept stands the very picturesque Great Organ, with its Choir in front. It has five towers, the two largest of which, supported by giants, stand at the sides, and the smallest occupies the centre. The Choir Organ has three towers, the least in the middle. Wood pipes, coloured red, are placed on each side of the Great Organ, with bad effect. The tone of the instrument is reedy and weak, and the wind short. The Accompaniment Organ, in an ordinary flat modern Gothic case, stands on the north side of the Choir. 1868.

LISIEUX.

ST. PIERRE (formerly the Cathedral).—A good sized organ, of a fair Gothic design, is on the north side of the Choir. It is played from the Stalls. There is no organ at the west end, which is rather unusual in a large French church. 1866.

ST. JACQUES.—The church was so dark that I could only make out that the organ, which stood at the west end of the church, had four towers, and the Choir in front, three. The case might have been an old one, half Flamboyant, and half Renaissance, or perhaps modern Gothic. 1866.

LYONS.

THE CATHEDRAL.—On the side of the Choir is a sweet-toned organ, a drawing of which is given in "Le Facteur d'Orgues." 1855.

RHEIMS CATHEDRAL

17TH AUGUST 1868.

ROUEN CATHEDRAL

21ST MAY. 1873

PARIS.

NOTRE-DAME. —A gigantic organ (the contents of which are by Cavaillé) stands at the west end of the church, in a fine old case of five towers, the largest of which are at each end of the case, and in the centre is the smallest, surmounted by a clock. In place of the usual Choir case is a console containing the keys, enabling the player to see down the nave. The organ is supported partly by a vaulting of stone, and partly by a wooden gallery, which, although no doubt perfectly correct, appears to me rather mean. Over the Stalls, on the north side of the Choir, is a small Accompaniment Organ, the wood-work of which does not harmonise well with the Stalls. 1868.

ST. EUSTACHE. —This church has three organs. At the west end is the Great Organ, with Choir in front, the case of which is of a rather unusual but handsome pattern. On the south side of the Choir is a good-toned Accompaniment Organ, in a plain case; and on the south side of the Lady Chapel is a little five-stop organ, with a plain case, composed of two flats. 1868.

RHEIMS.

THE CATHEDRAL. —The Great Organ stands in the north transept, in a very fine case, part Flamboyant and part Renaissance. It has five towers, the largest of which stands in the centre, the next in size at each end of the case, and the least occupy the intermediate positions. The Choir Organ in front has three towers, the tallest of which are at the ends. In the flats, of which there are four, two and two together, are ovals over the pipes, also fitted with pipes: the inner ovals had the smallest pipes I have ever seen put in front of an organ. The full tone of the instrument is very good; to be critical, a little wanting in diapason. The solo stops are good, the vox humana fairish, and the tremulant effective. The player knew well how to use the instrument. On each side of the case stand some pipes painted white, which are by no means so conspicuous as might be expected. The Choir Organ, for in this case it can hardly be called merely an Accompaniment Organ, stands on the south side of the Choir. Architecturally speaking, it stands in the nave, as the Choir extends three bays down the nave. It is modern Gothic, with a lofty tower in the centre, surmounted by a high pinnacle, and a sloping flat of pipes on each side. It has a good full tone; and, when I heard it, was exactly in tune with the large organ; so it was a great treat to hear one respond to the other. It has two rows of keys, and a pedal; and the stops were arranged on each side from the key-board down to the pedal, which cannot be convenient to the player. On a week day, I heard a very young man accompany the mass; he played very well and steadily, and when his services were not required, attended to the service in a manner which some organists might follow with advantage. Above the Great Organ stands a good rose window. 1868.

ST. ANDRÉ. —The organ stands on the south side of the Choir; it is in a flat case of carved oak, in the modern Norman style, but where they got their precedent, I do not know. However, it looked well, and the tone was good. 1868.

ST. RÉMI. —The organ is fitted into one of the north arches of the nave, part of which is used as the Choir, as in the cathedral. It has a plain flat front, and is played from the Choir Stalls. The stop handles are arranged in the same manner as those in the smaller organ in the cathedral. 1868.

ROUEN.

THE CATHEDRAL. —At the west end, under a grand rose window, stands one of the best organs in Normandy. Its gallery is supported by two internal buttresses of white stone, or marble, on each side of the grand entrance. It consists of five towers of five pipes each, the largest, which are the outside towers, being supported by giants, and surmounted by a statue. The two next towers have vases on their summits; and the centre tower, which is the least, is crowned with a clock. Between these towers stand four equal flats, with nine pipes each, which are perhaps the only failure in this grand case. The Choir in front has three towers, with five pipes each, surmounted with vases, the least in the centre, and two flats of nine pipes each. The culs-de-lampe have much open work about them. The organ gallery is concave in plan. The tone of the Great Organ is good, the shrill stops not being prominent, and the reeds not too loud. When I heard it, the player could not be called first-class. The Accompaniment Organ stands on the north side of the Choir; it has two gabled flats, with a narrow gable tower between, of modern Gothic work. Its tone is fair, but nothing particular. 1866, 1875.

CANTELEU.—The parish church is without an organ, but in the centre of the Choir stands a harmonium or American organ. It is a pity that a good church like this, in a wealthy suburb, is without a proper instrument. 1875.

ST. GEORGES DE BOSCHERVILLE.—A small village some little distance from the city, with a famous Norman church, which has a small old three-towered organ, with no Choir in front, standing in its west gallery. 1875.

ST. MACLOU.—The organ, which stands at the west end of the church, has four towers of five pipes each, the largest outside, overhanging the case. The two adjoining flats have seven pipes each, and the centre flat, which is divided in half, has nine pipes in its lower division, and thirteen in the upper, which is surmounted by a clock. The Choir in front, has three towers; the centre, which is the tallest, having seven pipes, the outer towers have five pipes, and the intermediate flats seven. The organ gallery is supported by grey marble columns, and on its south side has a very fine stone-staircase. The case has very elaborate Renaissance carving, and above it stands a good rose window. When I saw it in 1866, the organ had just been repaired, and the pipe-work was brilliant and had well-shaped mouths. When I saw it again in 1875, they looked very dull and out of condition. 1866, 1875.

NOTRE-DAME DE BON SECOURS has, at the west end, a modern French Gothic organ, with much gilding and plain pipes. The Choir Organ in front is very small, merely a screen in front of the player. Behind the Stalls, on the south aisle of the Choir, is a long low oak box, containing a small organ, the key-board of which is in the Choir Stalls. 1866.

ST. OUEN.—The organ stands in a grand case, in a gallery supported by white marble columns, at the west end of the church, with one of the finest rose windows in France over it. The great case has five towers with five pipes each, and four flats with seven each. The largest towers overhang the extremity of the case, and are surmounted by winged angels. The intermediate towers, which are half hexagons, have on the southern tower, the statue of St. Cecilia, and on the northern, one of King David. The centre tower, which is the smallest, has a figure which I could not make out. Query, St. Ouen? The Choir case has three towers of five pipes each, the least in the centre, with two flats of seven pipes. This organ has very good Renaissance carving about it. In a chapel on the north side of the Choir is a modern Gothic organ, the mouths of whose pipes are well formed. The key-board is in the Choir, and the trackers run under the side aisle. 1866, 1875.

ST. SEVER (on the south side of the river).—The organ in this church is curiously arranged. The west tower, which projects into the church, is faced with marble, the lower part of which consists of a large arch for the western door. It has on either side a round-headed recess, holding on one

ST MACLOU, ROUEN.

30TH MAY 1876.

ST OUEN—ROUEN

20TH MAY, 1875.

TROYES CATHEDRAL.

2ND SEPTR 1869

side a painting of St. Paul, and on the other, that of St. Peter. Above this is a large round arch, panelled with oak, with a small Choir Organ in front, and the upper part of the arch has pipes which follow its curve. Beyond this, can be seen a circular west window, with a flat of pipes underneath, with oak carving. On each side of this arch stand tall round arches, filled with pipe-work. 1875.

ST. VINCENT.—The aristocratic church of Rouen. The Tarif de Chaises beats any regulation for letting pews that I am aware of in England. At the west end is a Renaissance organ, with a Choir Organ in front, in fairish condition. On the north side of the Choir is an Accompaniment Organ, of the usual French Gothic pattern. 1866.

ST. VIVIEN.—In a gallery at the west end is a large organ, very similar to that in the Cathedral, the chief difference being, that in place of the intermediate towers, are pilasters surmounted by statues. The Choir Organ in front, which has three towers, projects very far from the gallery. On the north side of the Choir is a small organ of no particular style, consisting of three flats. 1875.

The three great organs in Rouen, in the Cathedral, St. Ouen, and St. Maclou, have cases of which any city or town may well be proud.

ST. LO.

ST. LO (formerly the Cathedral).—At the west end stands the organ, with its Choir in front. The case is a handsome one, in the old French style. It is not a large instrument, and its quality is noisy and bad. 1866.

ST. CROIX.—A modern Gothic organ stands at the west end, wanting the usual Choir Organ in front. 1866.

ST. RICQUIER.

THE ABBEY CHURCH.—A poor Picardy village, with a magnificent church, which has a good-looking organ, standing very high up in a vaulted gallery, at the west end. Its oak case has five towers, the largest at the ends, and the least in the centre, with an ordinary French Choir Organ in front. 1875.

STRASBURG.

THE CATHEDRAL.—I include this organ among French organs, as when I saw it, it belonged to France. Silberman's fine organ projects from the north triforium in the nave, its Gothic case, painted and gilded, is very handsome, and when I saw it, it looked as if it had just been put into good order. The case consists of a large central tower, with a flat on each side, beyond which are carved oak wings, with much gilding. Its Choir Organ, which projects in front, is very similar in pattern. Its quality is sweet, but a little muffled. However, I did not hear its full power. It was played by a lady, a good performer, who had presided at the instrument for some years. This is one of the best hanging organs I know, and without looking unwieldy, holds forty-two, a fair number of stops. It received considerable damage during the siege. 1868.

TROYES.

THE CATHEDRAL.—A fine organ stands at the west end of the church, under a grand Flamboyant rose window. It is proposed to remove the stone vault on which it stands, and to place the instrument, which is said to have been brought from the Abbey of St. Bernard, at Clairvaux, on iron girders, so as to allow the rose to be better seen. It has five towers, that in the centre containing the five largest pipes, surmounted by King David, with his harp; on each side of which is a flat containing nine pipes, then a little tower of five pipes, above which is an angel, who holds festoons of flowers, which come from the centre and end towers. Next comes a flat of eight pipes, beyond which are the end towers, with five large pipes, supported by giants, and crowned with a sitting angel, playing on a violin. The Choir Organ has three towers of five pipes each, the smallest tower, which is in the centre, carries a shield, and the end towers have each an angel. The base of the Choir Organ is stone, and on each side of the Great Organ case stand large wood pipes. The woodwork of the case is dark in colour, and the carving elaborate, with no gilding, and the pipes are plain. The Accompaniment Organ stands on the north side of the Choir, with a reversed key-board, played from the Stalls. Its pipes are plain, and the wood is left its natural colour. Its style is ultra-Gothic, minus the correct painting and gilding. 1869.

ST. *JEAN.*—At the west end is a fair-sized organ, with a Choir Organ before it, both having three towers, the smallest in the centre. 1869.

ST. *NIZIER.*—On the north side of the Choir stands an organ of modern Gothic work, with its key-board reversed. 1869.

ST. *RÉMI.*—An organ, the design of which is modern Gothic, stands at the west end. 1869.

The figures given at the end of each description, are the dates at which I saw the different instruments.

Unless it is stated that the pipes are gilded or painted, it is to be understood that the pipes in foreign organs are left their natural colour.

NOTES ON BELGIAN ORGANS.

ANTWERP.

HE *CATHEDRAL* (*Notre Dame*) has a grand instrument at the west end, standing in a gallery of black and white marble, supported by scagliola columns on black plinths. The gallery projects very much in front of the organ, so as to allow room for an orchestra. The centre tower contains seven pipes, and has on each side a bowed compartment of seven pipes, and next a flat of six pipes. These have over them a seated angel, so as to fill up the space between the centre and the next towers, which each contain five pipes. The next is a bowed compartment of three slender pipes, then a flat of three pipes, and at each end is a tower of five pipes surmounted by an angel playing on a large lute. The centre tower is surmounted by a sitting figure with angels, backed with carved work, above which is a winged angel holding a palm branch. The intermediate towers have each a high finial, with two angels holding trumpets. The oak work is elaborately carved, the claires-voies are gilt, and between the feet of the pipes carved work is inserted, which is also gilt. The mouths of the pipes, which, when I saw them, were in dirty condition, are gilt. The west window appears above the organ case, but the end of the Church is gloomy, and it is difficult to make out detail. I did not much admire the tone of this instrument. 1872.

THE *ENGLISH CHURCH* has a small organ in the west gallery, consisting of one manual with ten stops and no pedal, the tone bad. The oak case in the Renaissance style, with

ANTWERP CATHEDRAL
11TH SEPT. 1872.

ST PAULS ANTWERP

three towers, the smallest in the centre. Although the pipes of the outer towers are arranged in a semi-circle, the top is square, the gilded work at the top of the pipes making a sort of capital, which looks very well. 1872.

ST. GEORGE.—A new church, highly decorated, has at its west end a divided Gothic organ, not otherwise remarkable. 1872.

ST. JACQUES.—A semi-divided organ stands on a Choir Screen of black and white marble, the front towards the west, has on each side next the pillars of the church, a tower of seven pipes, then a small flat, beyond which is a still smaller flat. A low straight piece of oak carving joins this to similar work on the opposite side. The Choir front consists of a low centre, which has a bas-relief of St. Cecilia, below which is a small oval opening, which I fancy is useful to the organist. On each side of this is a flat of six pipes, a tower of five pipes, a flat of four pipes, and lastly, a tower of five pipes surmounted by figures. This portion of the case is low, and looks like a Choir Organ rather larger than usual. On each side of this work, comes a small flat of five pipes, then a larger flat of five pipes, and a tall tower of five pipes, all of which are crowned with figures and carving. The feet of the pipes in these last divisions commence about the level of the middle of those in the centre part. The mouths of the pipes are gilt, and have gilded work between their feet. This instrument is an excellent specimen of an organ standing on a Choir Screen, and so arranged as not to injure the view up and down the church. 1872.

ST. PAUL (Dominicans).—The organ, with its Choir Organ in front, said to be the finest in Belgium, and as far as the case and carving is concerned it well may be, stands at the west end of the Church, in a semi-circular gallery of black and white marble, with gilt balustrades. The rough outline of the case may be said to be a steep gable, with fantastic carvings above. The central portion stands on a very high plinth, the middle tower, which is crowned with a phœnix, standing above much curious carving, has five pipes carried on "pouts," and has on each side a double tier of eleven pipes, then an angular tower, crowned with a lyre and two angels, beyond which is a flat of seven pipes. All the wood-work is well carved, with a little gilding judiciously used. On each side of this central portion is a tower springing from a corbel, at a much lower level than the rest of the work, so that the tops of the pipes, which are five, standing on "pouts," are about level with the tops of the lowest pipes in the centre of the case. They are crowned with domes, from which dragons peep, and are surmounted by winged angels bearing trumpets. The Choir case has three angels on its central tower of seven pipes, on each side of which are two tiers of small pipes, and then an angular tower, surmounted by an angel. A wooden gallery joins the Choir case to the inner angle of the outer towers of the Great case, and a like gallery joins these towers to the walls of the nave. All this work overhangs the marble gallery below, and its curved supports are beautifully carved. The lower gallery contains the usual fittings of an orchestra, the pipes are quite plain and the leaf of their mouths is rounded, not sharp as in the Cathedral, or at St. Jacques, and no carving is introduced between their feet. 1872.

The wood of all these organs is dark, not black, oak, and the sculpture excellent.

BRUGES.

THE CATHEDRAL (St. Sauveur).—On the Choir Screen stands an elaborately designed organ. Its base is taller than usual, and the arrangement of pipes somewhat complicated. In the centre is a tower of seven pipes, with a flat on each side containing two tiers of pipes. Above the cornice of this work, rises in the centre a tall tower of seven pipes, crowned with much carved work, and surmounted by a large figure. On each side is a flat of pipes, with an angel playing on a trumpet in each corner. On each side of the organ stands a tower of five large pipes, with elaborate cornices and wings. That on the south side is surmounted by King David, and that on the north by St. Cecilia. These towers overhang the case, and are joined to the centre work by flats of seven pipes. The pipes are gilt in the English fashion, the front facing the Choir consists simply of panels of carved open work, with a Choir Organ in front, the pipes of which are gilt. 1872.

ST. ANNE.—On the Choir Screen stands a little organ, with gilt pipes and very elaborate carving. 1872.

ST. JACQUES.—On the Choir Screen is a handsome organ, with good carving. The side facing the Choir shows pipes in its two end towers only, the rest being filled in with open work tracery. 1872.

ST. JEAN (chapel in the hospital of).—The organ, not a very old instrument, stands in a second gallery, at the west end of the chapel, its pipes are gilt, and arranged somewhat in the German manner, showing a Great and Choir front in one case. 1872.

NOTRE DAME.—There is on the Choir Screen a very curious early Renaissance organ case, forming the base of the rood. Its pipes are not gilt, and it has a plain Choir Organ on its eastern side. 1872.

LES SŒURS DE CHARITÉ (chapel in the convent of).—In the west gallery is a small organ, standing flush with its front. It consists of a single flat of bright tin pipes, and the woodwork is painted white. 1872.

BRUSSELS.

STE. GUDULE.—At the west end is an ugly divided organ case, with very little work about it. In the front of its gallery is a hanging Choir Organ, of bad Gothic. On the south side of the Choir, stands a fair-sized harmonium. 1869.

NOTRE DAME DES VICTOIRES.—A Renaissance organ stands at the west end, the pipes plain, and the case dirty. It consists of a centre tower, two curved compartments, and two outer towers, supported by giants, and set at an angle of 45° with the front. The Choir Organ in front is very similar in pattern; the upper part of the Great Organ case has many carvings of musical instruments, &c., and a medallion bearing a head in the centre. 1872.

GHENT (Gand).

THE CATHEDRAL (St. Bavon).—A handsome organ stands at the junction of the north transept with the Choir, which has three towers with five pipes each; the two outside ones are supported by satyrs, and crowned with angels holding trumpets. On each side of the centre tower, are two flats of five pipes each, over which is much carving, with shields supported by angels. Over the centre tower is a small three-sided case, containing seven pipes in each compartment, surmounted with tabernacle work, on which is a figure on horseback, query, St. Bavon? The key-board of the organ is behind in a gallery, just under the vaulting of the north aisle of the Choir, which has a small Choir front facing the east; but I was told that this was really quite an independent instrument. The arches under the organ are cased with black and white marble, all the carving about the case is good, and dates from the seventeenth century. The case is of oak, but after the fashion of the country, painted oak colour. I objected to this, but was informed what could I expect, when they were in the habit of painting imitation marble on marble. The main case reaches about half-way up the triforium, and the upper case more than half-way up the

CATHEDRAL (ST BAVON) GHENT.

5TH OCT, 1872.

clerestory windows. The tone is good, and from its quality, I should say, has not been much altered from its original state. At High Mass I heard it very well played. The soft stops I could hardly hear, on account of the people perpetually moving in the Church. 1872.

THE BÉGUINAGE.—At the west end is an organ, not a very large one, with its Choir Organ planted just in front of it, or else inserted into the lower part of the case, German fashion. Its quality was not bad, and was fairly played by one of the Béguines, who was seated at the back of the instrument. 1872.

THE ENGLISH CHURCH (Temple Protestant).—In the west gallery is a small, poor-toned organ ; it has three towers, the least in the centre, which, however, stands higher than the others, from the plinth of the case curving up in the middle. On each side is a flat, with two tiers of pipes, and the cornice of the centre tower overlaps those of the other towers, which gives a crowded effect to the case. 1872.

ST. JACQUES.—The case of the organ, at the west end, is divided into three parts, the centre one being lower than the others. 1872.

ST. MICHAEL.—The modern organ at the west end of the church, is of a peculiar and very ugly design. 1872.

ST. NICOLAS.—At the west end is a modern Gothic organ, the front of which consists of a gable, with a lofty tower and pinnacle in the centre. 1872.

LIÉGE.

ST. JACQUES.—At the west end is a very pretty Renaissance organ. In the centre of the case is a large tower containing seven pipes, on each side of which is a flat, with a double tier of pipes, then a flat of four pipes, beyond which are semi-circular endings containing three pipes, supported by figures holding trumpets, and surmounted by tabernacle work. The lower part of the case is very tall, so that from the gallery to the feet of the pipes is nearly half the height of the instrument. In the front projects the Choir Organ, supported by a stone bracket. It consists of a central tower of seven pipes, with much carved work above, supporting a statue of St. Cecilia, with a flat on each side, and semi-circular ends, filled with pipes. All the work about this organ is very good, and by some it is considered the prettiest organ case in existence. 1863.

LOUVAIN.

ST. PIERRE.—The organ stands projecting from the east wall of the north transept, and fills the space between the clerestory and half way up the opening into the side aisles. The case consists of a tower of seven pipes in the centre, with tabernacle work on the top, crowned with St. Peter. On each side are tall flats, with a semi-circular pediment, beyond which are semi-circular ends, supported by brackets. It may be noted that the pipes in the semi-circular ends are very slender, and their feet are longer than their bodies. The Choir Organ in front is very similar in design. The carving about the case and gallery is nice, without being anything particular, and the tone fair, though rather deficient in power. 1872.

MECHLIN (Malines).

THE CATHEDRAL (St. Rumbold).—The organ, which stands at the west end, is an old ordinary-looking instrument. In the south aisle of the Choir is a modern Gothic organ. In the Cathedral of the Primate of Belgium one might expect that there would be finer instruments. 1872.

ST. JEAN.—At the west end is a modern Renaissance organ. A white plaster wall is brought so forward, that it stands flush with the front of the case, the effect of which is not good. 1872.

NOTRE-DAME.—In the south transept, over the Choir aisle arch, stands an organ with its Choir in front, good in tone, and in a very clean and good condition, so that I fancied it to be a new instrument. I was, however, told that it was old. The pipes were left their natural colour, and there was no gilding about the wood-work. It is a very pretty instrument on a moderate scale. 1872.

NOTES ON DUTCH ORGANS.

AMSTERDAM.

*IEUWE KERK.*—At the west end is a large organ, with double shutters, the lower half of the case being wider than the upper part. It is painted mahogany colour, as well as the Choir Organ in front. It is altogether a tasteless design. A second organ stands at the junction of the nave with the south transept; it is closed with shutters, and is a very good picturesque specimen of a small organ, as tasteful as the west organ is tasteless. 1872.

OUDE KERK.—At the west end, in a marble gallery, stands a fine organ, the wall behind which is painted black. The case is bronze colour, with white statues and decorations. The clairesvoies and the bases of the pipes have much gilding, and the mouths of the pipes are also gilt. It has five towers, the centre and the two outer of which are circular, the two others are angular. The central tower is surmounted by a black-faced clock, with white and gold ornaments. The southern circular tower has a statue of St. John, and the south angular tower a shield bearing a "ship proper." The north angular tower has the arms of the town, and the north circular tower a figure standing by an altar. The flats between the towers have each three tiers of pipes, the central tower two tiers, seven pipes in the lower, and nine in the upper. The angular towers have also two tiers, seven below and eleven above. The outer towers have seven pipes each. The Choir Organ has a central tower of seven pipes, with a flat on each side, containing two tiers of pipes, ten in each; then an angular tower of seven pipes, with half circles of ten pipes for a finish, above which are white recumbent figures. On the north side of the Church is a little organ closed with shutters, on which musical instruments are painted. 1872.

DELFT.

NIEUWE KERK.—A large organ at the west end, with a Choir Organ in front, said to have a very fine tone. The case is painted a light bright pink, and is very tasteless. 1872.

OUDE KERK.—At the west end is a large organ, with its Choir in front. Both have three towers, the largest in the centre. The pipes have gilt mouths, and the case is painted light salmon colour. It is a very similar design to the organ in the Nieuwe Kerk. 1872.

GOUDA.

JANSKERK (*St. John's*).—A fine organ with its Choir in front, painted a cold dark brown colour, stands in a marble gallery, at the west end of the Church. It is surrounded by a plaster curtain or mantle, coloured blue, with a dull red lining. It has three towers; the largest in the

OUDE KERK AMSTERDAM.

JANS KERK GOUDA

19TH SEPTR 1872.

ST BAVON HAARLEM.

23RD SEPTR 1872

ST JAN HERTOGENBOSCH

28TH SEPT 1872

centre has seven pipes, and is crowned with two angels, one of whom plays on a harp. On each side of the centre tower is a flat, with angels over them, the one playing a flute, the other a triangle; beyond which are angular compartments, joining the two outer towers, which are surmounted by angels bearing trumpets. Under the pipe-work stands coats-of-arms, blazoned and gilded. The front of the organ, which curves forward, is supported by four Corinthian columns, with gilt capitals. The centre tower of the Choir Organ has nine pipes, with a coat-of-arms over, supported by lions, on each side of which is a flat of pipes, beyond which are angular towers and curved ends. A large white and gold bracket supports this portion of the instrument. The balustrade of the gallery is wood-work, painted of the same colour as the organ, with coats-of-arms blazoned thereon, and having a handsome gilded cresting. The mouths of the pipes are gilt, and there is much gilding about the case, &c. The marbles of the gallery are grey and dove-coloured. 1872.

HAARLEM.

GROOTEKERK (St. Bavon).—This famous organ stands in a marble gallery at the west end of the Church, but the effect of its grand case is somewhat marred, by the Dutch want of taste, in the way the case is painted. The wall behind the instrument is painted a glossy black (the rest of the Church being whitewashed). The statues, coats-of-arms, &c., on the top of the instrument, are painted bright white, their bases grey marble, and the remainder of the case is painted with a light tint of dull pinkish drab. The mouths of the pipes and the carving at their tops and feet, are all brightly gilt. The support of the Choir Organ is bronze, with a large and two small gilded angels on it. Under the gallery is a white marble allegory, which I will not attempt to explain, and the entire top of the case, except the outer towers, is crowned with a mass of carving, with the arms of the town supported by lions. The central tower consists of two tiers, the lower of seven, the upper of nine pipes. On each side is a narrow flat, divided into five compartments, the next but one to the top being occupied by a statue playing on a musical instrument, and the rest filled with small pipes. Next are angular towers, with their pipes arranged in the same mode as the centre, beyond which is a flat, containing two tiers of pipes, above which is a niche with a statue. Beyond this are the two outer towers of seven great pipes each, the feet of which commence at a much lower level than the rest of the pipes, so that the summit of these towers is not so high as the rest of the instrument. That on the south side is crowned with King David, and that on the north with a figure, but whom it represents I never could find out. Outside the great tower, on tall pedestals, stand angels with trumpets. The Choir Organ has its tallest tower of seven pipes in the centre; a flat of three tiers of pipes on each side; then an angular tower of seven pipes, and curved ends. These last are surmounted by sitting figures. The balustrade of the gallery has some elaborate carved open work above it, and its supporting columns are of some sort of dark marble. The general tone of the instrument is very good, but the vox humana is bad. The player, though he could hardly be called first-rate, was very skjlful in showing off the quality of the instrument. All the fittings about the key-board are clumsy; the black keys are topped with tortoiseshell. The cornices of the towers greatly overhang, but the flats between being small in proportion to the towers, and the intricacy of the general forms, prevent the usual ill effect. 1872.

HERTOGENBOSCH (Bois-le-Duc).

ST. JANSKIRK.—The organ case at the west end of this church is perhaps the finest in Europe. The oak wood-work is very dark, and profusely carved, without any gilding, and is in a good state of polish. The top of the case from the ground is about one hundred feet. The pipes, which, when I saw them, were in very bright condition, have their mouths gilded. The centre pipes of each tower have a pattern beaten upon their surface, and are gilt, with the exception of the lower one on the centre tower, which is only partially gilt. The centre tower, which is surmounted by a clock, under which is the Dance of Death, or some such subject, has two tiers of pipes, seven below and eleven above. On each side of this is a flat, divided into two tiers, which contain, in the lower compartment, what may be called five double pipes, or perhaps, more accurately speaking, it has ten pipes, with their feet joined together, the heads of the lower ones standing on the plinth, and the upper ones in their usual position. I could not see how these pipes were supplied with wind, and I have a strong idea that they are dummies. In the upper part were six double pipes arranged in the same manner, and above are niches, figures, columns, and pediments. Next come two angular towers, with a lower tier of seven, and an upper tier of eleven pipes. And to finish the organ, instead of the great towers, as at Haarlem, are two large flats corbelled out from the sides of the instrument, containing five large pipes, and sloping towards the wall behind. These are crowned with fantastic pyramids. The Choir Organ in front has over its centre tower, which contains five pipes, a figure of St. John with his Eagle, on each side of which is a flat with seven small pipes, in its lower compartment, and in its upper compartment six double pipes, similar to those in the Great Organ. Beyond this, is an angular tower of seven pipes, with a vase on its summit, and a small return compartment of pipes, joining the case to the gallery, which is of elaborately carved oak, and supported by two grey stone pillars. I did not hear the instrument, but was told it was nearly as good as Haarlem. 1872.

ROTTERDAM.

GROOTEKERK (St. Laurence).—At the west end stands a very large organ. The centre tower, which is ninety feet high from the ground, and is crowned with an angel holding a trumpet, has two tiers of pipes, the lower containing fifteen, and the upper nineteen. On each side is a flat with three tiers of pipes; then a flat of four tall pipes; and at each end a tower surmounted with a vase, containing five pipes, belonging to the thirty-two feet stop, and which look very long and thin, as they have a rather narrow scale. On a bracket, outside the north tower, is an angel playing on the lute; on the south side, one who plays on the flute. The buffet, or lower part of the case, rises in a curve to the centre; the Choir Organ in front, has its tallest tower in the centre, surmounted by three angels; next to which is a flat of two tiers of pipes, seven in each; then a flat of four pipes, and at each end a tower of seven pipes. The organ loft is white, and supported by eight Ionic columns, with bronze capitals, and the culs-de-lampe of the three towers of the Choir Organ are also bronze. The pipes had gilt mouths, the wood-work was all brown oak, much carved with festoons of flowers, and sham curtains for claires-voies. I heard the organ at a week-day evening service, the tone was good, but wanting in fulness. I suspect I did not hear the full power. 1872.

UTRECHT.

THE CATHEDRAL (St. Martin).—The organ stands where the nave of the Cathedral, which has fallen down, commenced, and beneath it is a pulpit with a square sounding-board. It is a new instrument, of a light yellow colour, in modern German Gothic. The great case consists of three equal towers, of seven pipes each, the centre surmounted by King David, and the others by pinnacles of open-work; and an open-work gallery joins these together, beneath which are two flats,

ST LAWRENCE (GROOTE KERK) ROTTERDAM.
17TH SEPT. 1872.

the upper part of which is an elaborate Gothic window, the background of dark blue, with four and twenty pipes in each, divided by the mullion of the window. The Choir Organ consists of a large gable, of open Gothic work, between two pinnacled towers of seven pipes each. In the centre is a sort of Gothic window, with two flats of twelve pipes, and on each side, a flat with a double tier of pipes, adjoining the towers. A gallery, decorated with quatre-foils, connects the two organs. The mouths of the pipes are gilt, and there is some gilding about the case, which cannot be called a handsome one, as it violates all the rules of what a good organ case should be. 1872.

ST. NICOLAS.—At the west end is a very curious little old organ, with a quaint Choir Organ in front, supported by a single square column. It consists of two flat overhanging towers, with an angular centre tower, rather taller, all crowned with Gothic pinnacle work. The flats joining these towers, which rise to the centre tower, have each fourteen pipes, above which are a set of pipes with two bodies, two mouths, and two feet; in fact two pipes joined together at their feet. I could not see how they could be supplied with wind. The Choir Organ in front has three angular towers, with no flats between them; the centre, the tallest, has seven pipes; the others have five pipes on their outer side, and on their inner side pipes similar to those in the upper part of the flats of the Great Organ. A small curved compartment on each side, completes this case. The mouths of the pipes are gilt, and there is some gilding about the case. It was dusk when I saw this organ, which I am sure is worth a careful examination, as there is much about it that is old and curious. 1872.

In the museum of the Archbishop are some painted shutters belonging to some old organ, the bass being David playing before the Ark, and the treble, David playing before Saul. 1872.

NOTES ON GERMAN ORGANS.

COBLENTZ.

T. CASTOR.—A west end organ, with a rather elaborate case, which has the German peculiarity of the Great Organ case having, under the usual pipes, pipes as of a Choir Organ. I imagine this organ was played from the side. 1869.

COLOGNE.

THE CATHEDRAL.—The organ stands in a wooden gallery at the end of the north transept. The case, which is of a confused design, is not good; part of the work is old. The Choir Organ pipes show, after the German manner, in the lower part of the Great Organ. case. The tone was fair, but it was not sufficient for the building, and there was no striking quality about it. 1869.

This organ is to be replaced by an enormous instrument, with at least 100 registers.

THE MINORITES.—At the west end stands a large organ, said to be the best in the city, and the little I heard at vespers was good. The pipes were very dull and dirty. The case, painted white, and relieved with gilding, is very curious. It stands right across the church, flush with the front of the gallery, on which it stands. At each end is a projecting tower, supported by figures, and containing seven pedal pipes. In the middle of the gallery is the Choir Organ, the centre tower of which is supported by a figure. Arches are thrown from this organ to the towers on each side, on which, and above the Choir Organ, stands the Great Organ case, a confused mass of angular and round towers, curved and broken pediments, &c.

The player sat under the arch on the north side, but I could not see the precise position of the key-board. The case was broad and shallow, and stood about one bay clear of the west window, which was large and handsome. 1869.

FRANKFORT.

THE CATHEDRAL.—When I saw this church, it was under repair after the fire, and the only organ in it was a small modern Gothic instrument, which was evidently a temporary erection. 1869.

FREIBURG-IM-BRESGAU.

THE CATHEDRAL.—The Great Organ is a hanging one, and is pendent above a pillar half way down the north side of the nave. It was built in 1515, and repaired in 1818. It has two flat towers of seven pipes each, the largest being outside, with a V flat of 20 pipes between, above which is a statue of the Virgin and Child, with scroll work all gilt. The towers overhang the base on each side. The Choir Organ, which consists of a flat of nine pipes, between two flat towers of five pipes each, hangs in front of the organ gallery, which is a semi-octagon, with gilt open-work, and its corbel terminates in an angel playing a trombone. This organ is only played at the great festivals; the tone is said to be good. Showing under the south-east arch of the choir, is an organ placed on a platform, which fills up one bay of the south aisle. Its date is about 1700. It has three flat towers of five pipes each, the smallest in the centre with one pipe in each angle, so as to make the towers project slightly in front of the two flats, which contain ten pipes each. On each side of the case is a wooden screen containing a wheel window. The towers are crowned with open Gothic pinnacles, and the style is a mixture of Gothic and Renaissance. The organ gallery has open wood work about it. Three bellows stand in a loft on a level with the organ pipes. The blower stands on a floor level with the organ gallery, and works the bellows by means of ropes coming through the floor, as if he were ringing bells. The organ has but one manual, C C to f³ fifty-four notes, and a pedal from CCC to D, fifteen notes. Its naturals are black and its sharps white. Its contents are :

Principal	.	.	.	.	4	Fagot Man. bass	.	.	8	Principal	.	.	.	.	8	Mixtur	.	.	5 ranks
Viole de Gambe	.	.	.	8	Waldfloete disc¹	.	.	8	Cornet	.	.	(Qy.)	8	1				
Quinte	.	.	.	.	3	Octav bass	.	.	8	Bourdon	.	.	.	.	8	2 } Draw stops without names.		
Octave	.	.	.	.	2	Sub-bass	.	.	10	Floete	.	.	.	.	4	3		

The Nave Organ in this Church is a very good specimen of a hanging organ. 1869.

ST. ——.— A Church (near the statue of Schwartz) the name of which I omitted to learn. At the west end in a very deep gallery, supported by many columns, is an organ of brown wood, in the Teutonic taste of the seventeenth century. It has a large centre tower, with a small flat of little pipes on each side ; then a painted tower, beyond which is a wing of pipes, looking like the open shutter of a tryptich, the largest pipe being outside. The Choir Organ, which stands well away from

FREIBURG IM BRESGAU

21 SEPT 1869

the great case, has three towers, the least in the centre, with flats between. All the ornaments are painted white, and the pipes stand their natural heights, with carved work so fitted as to stand clear of them. The irregular effect is peculiar. 1869.

INNSBRUCK.

HOFKIRCHE.—In the Silver Chapel is an organ said to have belonged to Philippina, who died in 1580. It is a curious old instrument, with a moutre of cedar, and all the work is very rough and clumsy. 1855.

THE JESUITS' CHURCH.—At the west end stands an organ in a heavily designed case, painted white, with a very small Choir before it, not higher than the front of the gallery. In the centre of the Great Organ is a fanciful arrangement of pipes, forming a perspective. I may mention that this Church has its flat roof painted so as to represent three domes, a clever deception on first entering the Church. In the Tyrol flat towers with seven pipes are common. 1855.

MAGDEBURG.

THE CATHEDRAL.—At the west end is an organ having plain metal pipes, and decorated with much bad modern Gothic work. 1863.

MAYENCE.

THE CATHEDRAL.—In the north gallery of the western transept, stands a small organ of last century work. It has two fronts, the chief looking towards the west, and the other to the north. The case, which is white, has much ornament about it. As the Cathedral was under repair at the time I saw it, there may be some larger instrument in it which I did not see. 1869.

MUNICH.

THE JESUITS' CHURCH.—The only note I took of the organ was that it had a very low Choir Organ, not higher than the front of the gallery. 1863.

PRAGUE.

THE CATHEDRAL.—The organ at the west end is very much divided. In the lowest gallery stands a sort of Choir Organ, above which in another gallery stands a still smaller case, and again, above this, is the Great Organ, which is a divided one. On the right of the entrance, in a small side chapel, is the rudest organ I have yet met with. It is closed with shutters, and a sort of screen of wood pipes stands behind the player. 1863.

THE MONASTERY OF STRAHOW.—The organ stands at the west end of the Church, and another at the north side of the choir, to match which on the south side is a painting of a similar organ. 1863.

SCHWARZ.

PFARRKIRCHE.—This is a curious double Church, with two naves and chancels, standing side by side. The organ stands at the west end, and the Choir Organ in front goes round the pillar common to both naves. 1863.

NOTES ON SWISS ORGANS.

BERNE.

HE CATHEDRAL.—The organ stands at the west end. It was originally built in 1727, and was repaired and greatly enlarged in 1847 by F. Hass. It contains fifty-six stops and has four rows of keys. I did not like the tone of the instrument, it was loud and hard, the reeds and mixtures too prominent, the trumpet stops but ordinary, and the vox humana bad. The organ was played well by the organist, who gave us but a short exhibition of his skill. The old case is retained, and consists of five towers of seven pipes each, separated by flats of four pipes each. The largest tower is in the centre, surmounted with a large vase and many carved flowers. The next towers in size are at the extremity of the instrument, surmounted by angels playing on musical instruments. The least towers stand in the centre of the intermediate spaces, surmounted by large vases and carvings of musical instruments. The gallery in which it stands is modern Gothic. 1863.

COIRE.

THE DOM (*St. Lucius*).—At the west end is an organ, erected in 1815, containing thirteen stops, one manual, and a pedal. The case is painted brown, picked out with green, and is certainly ugly. It stands before a plain round-headed window, and may be called a divided organ. At each end of the case is a compartment with an ogee top, containing seven pipes, next to which is a compartment with a curvilinear top and fourteen pipes, leaving the centre of the organ above the impost clear for about the width of the window, except for a small frame, with double ogee top, containing a single row of small pipes. On the north side of the case are posted wooden trumpet tubes, and the tubes of a similar stop appear over the smaller case on the north side. The bellows are in a chamber on the north side of the organ, and a wooden tube brings the wind down to it. I was told that behind the high altar was a very old small organ, but I could not see it as the Church was under repair. 1869.

FREIBURG.

ST. NICOLAS—This famous organ stands in a modern Gothic gallery at the west end of the Church. The outline of the case (which is also modern Gothic) is a large gable, having in the centre a tall tower, with two tiers of seven pipes each. The compartments on each side of this have each two tiers of pipes, between which is wood work, containing a rose of Gothic tracery. Beyond this is a tall tower of five pipes, then a flat of tall pipes, and the organ terminates at each end with a tower of five pipes. All the work is crowned with pinnacles and tabernacle work, the wood-work is pale oak, with gilding about it. Although intended to be a handsome case I do not quite like it. The tone of the organ is good, especially the echo, and the vox humana has a great renown. 1868.

GENEVA.

THE CATHEDRAL.—The Great Organ, at the west end of the building, has a modern Gothic case, with five towers, the largest in the centre, and the least at the ends. It is not handsome. This organ was built by Merklin and Schulse, of Brussels and Paris. It has forty-six stops, three manuals, and pedal. Its quality was loud, and wanting in diapason tone. The reeds are monotonous, and the vox humana bad. The organist was a pupil of the late Herr Vogt, the organist at Freiburg, who was one of the best of European organists. 1868.

THE ENGLISH CHURCH has, in its west gallery, a poor-toned organ, in a dingy-coloured Gothic case, consisting of three towers, the largest in the centre, separated by flats, with two tiers of pipes. 1868.

THE GREAT ST. BERNARD.

THE HOSPICE.—The organ, which stands at the west end, appears to have been brought forward, as the colour of the wood-work at the side shows, the front panels looking older than those behind. The bellows stand in a high box on the north side of the instrument, and are dated 1812, which I fancy must mean the date of some reparation, as the case looks older. The front consists of three flat towers, of five pipes each, with flats between. On the centre tower, which is the tallest, is a standing figure, and above the side towers are seated figures. It has black naturals, and the sharps have an ivory line down them. The key-board has four octaves and two notes, C C to D, no lower, C C². The pedal-board is one octave and four notes, C C C to E, no lower, C C C², with an iron bar for a rest over them. When I heard the organ it was much out of order, and the wind was leaky. The full organ tone was still good.

CONTENTS.

Prestant.	Viola.	Basse.	Doublet.	Clarion.
Bourdo'.	Tierce.	Cornet.	Viola.	Tremb'.
Nasard.	Tromp.	Flute.	Tromp.	

The gallery which holds the above is supported by pillars, and the paintings in the compartments, beginning from the left, are a Pot of Lilies, a Pelican and her Piety, King David, Instruments of Music (this is the centre compartment), St. Cecilia, a Burning Cloud and a Pot of Lilies. 1868.

LUCERNE.

HOFKIRCHE, CHURCH OF ST. LEODEGAR (St. Leger).—The fine old organ of this Church stands at the west end, and was greatly added to and repaired, by M. Haass, who lives close to the Church, and who completed his work in 1862. It now contains seventy sounding stops, all of which are throughout, none of the metal stops having the lowest octave in wood, nor are closed pipes used instead of open. There are four manuals and a pedal. The case consists of five compartments. The centre, which is by far the largest, holds the five lower pipes (of pure tin) of the thirty-two foot open, which have very short feet. On each side of this, is a compartment of nine pipes with very long feet. The outer flats have nine good-sized pipes, with feet of average length. These two last compartments stand at an angle with the other three compartments. All the pipe-work is bright tin; the wood-work brown oak, with a quantity of fantastic carving. There is a peculiar look about this front, it is a Screen, not a case to the organ. The Great Organ has a good tone, the old tone, without the bray of the reeds, which one so often gets in modern instruments. The imitation of thunder is fair, the full power of the organ good, the trumpets telling well, without being overpowering. The vox humana was very good : "Quelle soprano!" exclaimed a French lady behind me, as the organist was showing it off. When the swell of the vox humana is closed, and the tremulant drawn, it makes an excellent vox angelica, very soft and good, but trembling a little too much, and the tone is so hushed, that people must be very quiet in the Church to hear it. The organist, when I heard this instrument, was a showy player, but he accompanied the Mass in a very efficient manner, and with great judgment. A fugue be played at the end of the service had only one fault, that was, its shortness. 1863, 1869.

THE ENGLISH CHURCH has a modern Gothic organ at its west end. At each end of the case is a tall tower, of seven pipes, with pinnacles of open work. Next is a gabled compartment, and the centre consists of two flats, having a horizontal cornice. Much tawdry gilt-work is spread about the case. The Choir Organ has three compartments, with a flat cornice and much gilded carvings. I expect this case is a sham, and is merely a buffet for the keys, as on the top of it was a music-desk, and the player sat with his back to the Great Organ. I did not like the tone of the instrument, which was but fair. 1869.

NOTES ON ITALIAN ORGANS.

BELLAGGIO.

RIVATE CHAPEL OF VILLA MELZI.—Just inside the chapel, is a "grinder" with four or five stops, in a cabinet case. 1869.

CHIAVENNA.

SAN LORENZO.—At the west end is an organ of pale-coloured varnished wood, with gilt ornaments. It consists of a round arched centre, with flat wings. The gallery in which it stands, is level with the capitals of the nave arches, and is carried out on each side as far as the first pillars, making two excellent side galleries for a divided choir. 1869.

COMO.

THE CATHEDRAL.—The two organs stand under the eastern arches of the nave, in galleries, which stand on elliptical arches, borne on four columns. Their cases, the whole of which are gilt and burnished, consist of two Corinthian or composite columns, bearing a broken pediment. The pipe-work is covered with a blue curtain. A statue of the Virgin forms the centre ornament of the north organ, and on the southern instrument is one of a bishop. The back of this latter instrument has a Renaissance screen, of curious lattice-work, brightly gilt. That of the north organ is simply plain wood. There are seats and music desks in the gallery in the front of each organ for the choristers. For antiphonal music, nothing can be better than the arrangement of these instruments. The position at Milan is good, but this is preferable. 1869.

ISOLA BELLA.

IN THE CHURCH (not in the Chapel of the Palace), in a gallery at the west end, stands an organ, in a white painted case, picked out with colour, consisting of merely two pilasters, supporting a low pediment. The pipes, which looked quite new, are bright tin, the tallest standing in the centre, and the smallest half-way between the centre and the sides of the case, against which stand tall pipes, so that the arrangement is somewhat like a W. The pipes show their real heights, their tops all being below the top of the case, without any bad effect from want of symmetry ; if anything, the effect is good. Some wood bourdons, standing outside the instrument on each side, show that at some time or other additions have been made to it. I may mention that it is common in Italy for the pipes to show their real heights, and for the montre to be covered with curtains or blinds, or sometimes with pictures, when the instrument is not in use. 1869.

MADONNA DI TIRANO.

IL SANTUARIO.—An organ with a very fine case, well carved on both sides, stands across the transept, the montre covered by a large picture.

MILAN.

IL DUOMO (the Cathedral).—On each side of the choir stand two fine organs, externally both alike; the back and front of each is very similar, the latter having more ornaments. Their bases on the choir side, are faced with dark wood, that facing the aisle is marble. Their montres are closed with painted shutters, their choir front has two Corinthian or composite columns, with a flat entablature. The front towards the aisle, has similar columns, and a broken carved pediment. Each organ is surmounted with a circular temple, with statues in the niches, and covered with a dome, with a statue on its summit. All the work about the instrument is gilt, the pipes are left their natural colour and their correct heights, and their tops do not reach the carved work among which they stand. The five largest are arranged in the centre, and the compartment on each side of these has two tiers, with nine pipes each. Beyond them is an outer compartment of five pipes. I did not think the quality of these instruments so good as Mr. Hopkins states them to be in his work on "The Organ." The quality of the northern organ was sweet, but lacking in power. The voicing of the flute was very good. The vox humana (said to be a flute stop, as reeds are not permitted by the Ambrosian rite) was very suggestive, and had a peculiar intonation, which was very pleasant, although not a good imitation of the human voice. The player's style was very operatic, and the singing resembled the old Madrigal style. I like the full tone of the southern organ, rather better than that of the northern one. It was weak for the large building in which it stands, and more diapason and pedal work was much wanted. I did not hear the solo stops of this organ, but there was "the old tone" in the instrument, which was pleasant to hear. 1869.

SAN AMBROGIO.—The organ has a long low case of several compartments painted white, and the montre is covered with dark blue curtains. It stands close to the dome, over the south transept, in what was originally the women's gallery. 1869.

SAN GIOVANNI IN LATERAN.—The organ in a case, consisting of two pilasters with entablature over a round arch, with a curtain concealing the pipes, stands at the west end of the Church. 1869.

SAN LORENZO.—An octagon church, has in the gallery on its south-east side a small organ in a white and gold case, consisting of a round arched centre, and two flat sides, looking somewhat like a handsome wardrobe. Green curtains covered the pipes. In a rather large chapel attached to this Church, stood a grand pianoforte, an old instrument, but evidently still in use. This is the only place in which I ever recollect seeing a piano in a church. 1869.

SANTA MARIA DELLE GRAZIE.—This Church has a dome in its centre, the base of which expands into a square, on the east side of which, right and left of the choir, two similar organs stand in galleries, having much gilding. The cases, which are of dark wood, have flat tops, bearing two angels with trumpets, and raised carved work in the centre. The pipes were covered with a curtain, and the ornaments in the front and sides of the cases were gilt. 1869.

SANTA MARIA PODONE.—This little old Church has in a painted gallery at its west end, an organ in a square case, with a curtain, as usual, drawn over the pipes. 1869.

SAN ———, (*in the Via di Giadini*), has at its west end, standing in a rococo gallery, an organ of the same style, in a polished, and much gilded brown case, which is either new, or else lately done up. The pipes are covered with curtains, and the design of the case consists of three compartments, the outer ones having round arches. The central compartment is surmounted by a confusion of curved lines, having the appearance of a drawing-room looking-glass, slightly overdone with ornament. 1869.

CONCLUSION.

 HAVE now given to my readers the full substance of all the notes I have made on the various organs I have seen, and regret that they were not all taken so systematically as I could have wished, for when I began them, they were simply memoranda, to assist my own recollection, and I had no intention of ever publishing them. But as my note book kept filling with accounts of organs, and my portfolio with sketches, I could but feel that I should like others to have the use of the information I had accumulated. My descriptions are simply taken from what I saw, and not extracts from books, or the accounts of friends, and the sketches have all been made on the spot, no doubt with some errors, but still the evidence of an eye-witness is better than second-hand information, gathered from sources that may be sometimes inaccurate, and, being copied over and over again, come to be handed down as facts. Should this little work in any way tend towards the improvement of THE ORGAN, I shall be amply repaid for the time and trouble spent upon it.